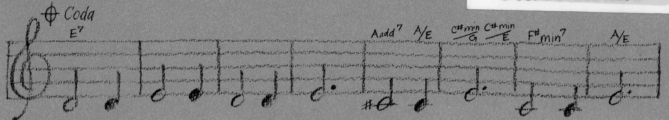

We are pirates in the tub - Yo

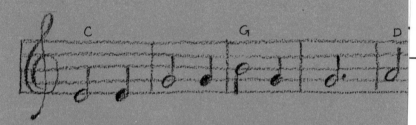

We see clouds that look like fish - Firs

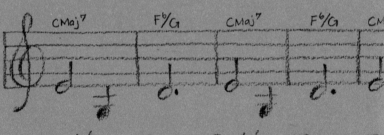

Golden Bear, Golden Bear - I

Dreaming dreamy dreams at night - Golden Bear tucked in tight.

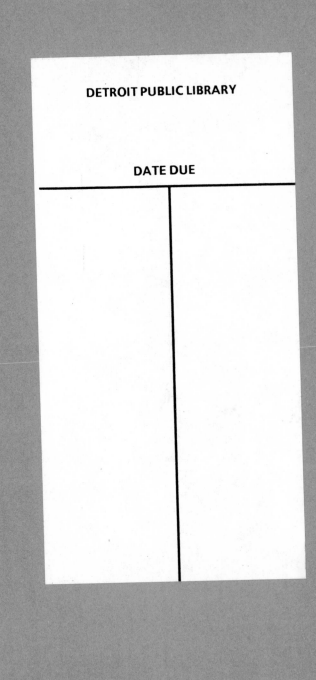

DETROIT PUBLIC LIBRARY

DATE DUE

Golden Bear

Golden Bear

Ruth Young

ILLUSTRATIONS BY
Rachel Isadora

Viking

VIKING

Published by the Penguin Group

Viking Penguin, a division of Penguin Books USA Inc.,

375 Hudson Street, New York, New York 10014, U.S.A.

Penguin Books Ltd, 27 Wrights Lane, London W8 5TZ, England

Penguin Books Australia Ltd, Ringwood, Victoria, Australia

Penguin Books Canada Ltd, 10 Alcorn Avenue, Toronto, Ontario, Canada M4V 3B2

Penguin Books (N.Z.) Ltd, 182–190 Wairau Road, Auckland 10, New Zealand

Penguin Books Ltd, Registered Offices: Harmondsworth, Middlesex, England

First published in 1992 by Viking Penguin, a division of Penguin Books USA Inc.

3   5   7   9   10   8   6   4   2

Text copyright © Ruth Young, 1992
Illustrations copyright © Rachel Isadora, 1992
Music and lyrics copyright © Ruth Young, 1992
All rights reserved
Music transcription and lettering by Kathy McNicholas

Library of Congress Cataloging-in-Publication Data
Young, Ruth, 1946-
Golden Bear / Ruth Young ; illustrations by Rachael Isadora.
p.   cm.
Summary: Golden Bear and his human companion learn to play the violin,
talk to a ladybug, make mudpies, wish on stars, and dream together.
ISBN 0-670-82577-8
[1. Bears—Fiction. 2. Friendship—Fiction.] I. Isadora, Rachael, ill. II. Title.
PZ7. Y877Go   1992   [E]—dc20   89-24843   CIP   AC

Printed in Hong Kong
Set in 22 point Goudy Catalog

To Lucia
—R.Y.

For Gillian and Nicholas
—R.I.

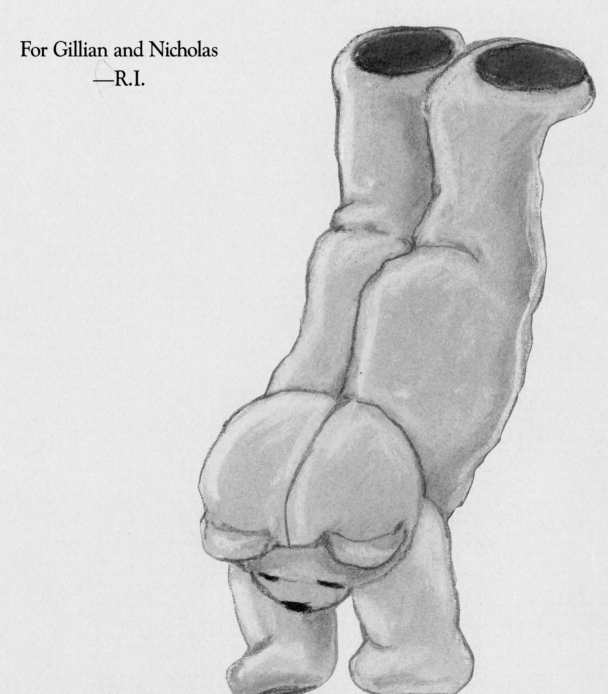

Golden Bear, Golden Bear,
I have seen him everywhere:

Dancing up the golden stair

Rocking in my rocking chair

Playing on the violin
Balanced underneath his chin

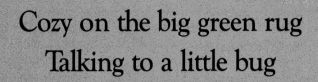

Cozy on the big green rug
Talking to a little bug

Skating fast on silver ice
Tracing perfect circles twice

Making snowmen in the snow

Watching tulips start to grow

In the garden planting seeds
Making mudpies, pulling weeds

Talking on the telephone
With me when I'm all alone

We are pirates in the tub
Yo, ho, ho! Scrub, scrub, scrub

We see clouds that look like fish
First star out—make a wish

Dreaming dreamy dreams at night
Golden Bear tucked in tight.

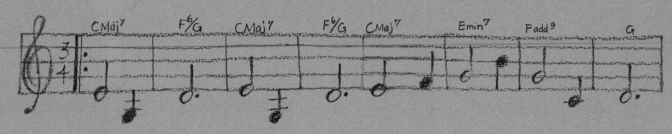

Golden Bear, Golden Bear, I have seen him Every-where -
Playing on the vio —— lin   Balanced under-neath his chin —
In the garden planting seeds - Making mud pies, pull-ing weeds-

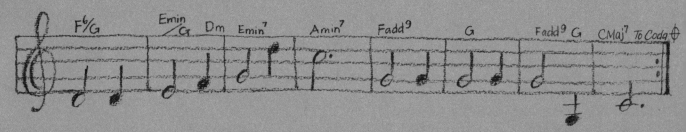

Dancing up the golden stair, Rocking in my rocking chair
Cozy on the big green rug, Talking to a little bug
Talking on the tele — phone With me when Im all a—lone

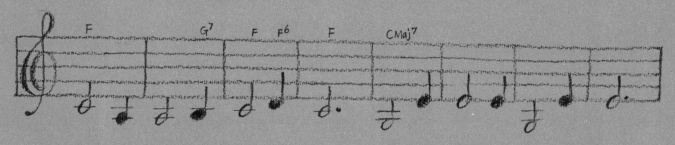

Skating fast on silver ice - Making perfect circles twice

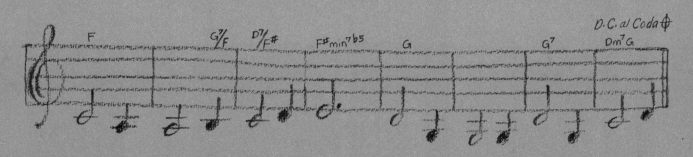

Making snowmen in the snow-Watching tulips start to grow—